Download a free The
Bear Arms lesson plan at
www.ClassicalLearner.com

Little Bears listen here,
To a story about more than rabbits & deer.
The world can be a tricky place,
So listen, look, smell, touch, & taste.
Here is what your parents meant,
About your Right to self-defense.

Charisma Cat's beauty was a sight to see,
But light revealed eyes filled with greed.
The water, trees, plants, the wealth,
She wanted the forest for herself.
She schemed to make other animals weak,
Especially those armed to the teeth.

She convinced all of the local roosters,
To report of skunks going bazookas.
Skunk attacks left & right,
More attacks, day & night.
The animals didn't know what to think,
But smart Bears said "this story stinks."
Roosters yelled "skunks must disarm,"
"A skunk that can't spray can do no harm."
Animals chanted in the streets,
"The smell of skunk violence reeks."

The Daily News

Skunks are bad

The skunks signaled to the crowd, "Skunks having stink is no longer allowed."

Roosters yelled "the goats are bad,"
"Disarm now, we animals are mad."
Gullible goats filled with shame,
Gave up their horns to show they'd changed.
The sacrifice worked like a charm,
Many animals would disarm.

The mountain lions gave up their teeth,
While the hummingbirds surrendered their beaks.
The porcupines removed their spikes,
and wild hogs didn't think twice.
Charisma Cat had one more trick,
Deception that will make you sick.

The roosters reported of a rabbit attacked,
The poor bunny had Bear claw marks on her back.
The animal community was blinded with rage,
"These Bears, they should be in a cage."
Charisma Cat called for all to disarm,
"Declawed Bears can do no harm."

The falcons were quick to hand over their talons,
A fox with no tail is a fox that can't balance.
The horses elected to surrender their shoes,
but Bears are careful with the choices they choose.
The Bears would not relinquish their claws,
They kept them attached to their big, strong, Bear paws.

Bear arms

The animals were about to discover,
Charisma Cat's plan to plunder.
With talons, teeth, pines, & skunk smell,
One by one the animals fell.
The animals wished they could take back,
The weapons Charisma Cat used to attack.

Goats, hogs, & birds locked away,
Most of the forest was conquered in days.
Charisma Cat had arrived at the den,
The Bears were ready to fight till the end.
A claw, a bite, & one Big Bear hook,
Charisma Cat was frightened & shook.

The cat tucked her tail & scurried away,
The Bears did not care what she had to say.
Read this again, for you have been warned,
Do not surrender that with which you were born.
Little Bears learn from your dads & your moms,
You have a God given Right to Bear arms.

Download a free The Right to Bear Arms lesson plan at www.ClassicalLearner.com

Have you read
Good Bears Always Tell the Truth?

Available on Amazon